BLOOD ALLIANCE SERIES
CHASTELY BITTEN
ROYALLY BITTEN
REGALLY BITTEN
REBEL BITTEN
VICIOUSLY BITTEN
KINGLY BITTEN
CRUELLY BITTEN
FOREVER BITTEN

BLOOD ALLIANCE WORLD
BLOOD DAY
BLOOD CITY

FOREVER BITEN

LEXI C. FOSS

This is a work of fiction. Names, characters, places, and incidents are either the product of the author's imagination or are used fictitiously, and any resemblance to actual persons, living or dead, business establishments, events, or locales is entirely coincidental.

Forever Bitten

Editing by: Outthink Editing, LLC

Proofreading by: Katie Schmahl

Cover Art and Design by Tairelei (https://www.instagram.com/tairelei/)

Published by: Ninja Newt Publishing, LLC

Print Edition

ISBN: 978-1-68530-395-2

AI Disclaimer: This book does not contain any elements of AI content. All art was designed by real artists, and all of the words were written by the author.

FOREVER BITTEN

A Blood Alliance Novella

LEXI C. FOSS

Forever Bitten is not a novella or even a short story. It's just a collection of bonus scenes that happened to be lingering in my mind after finishing *Cruelly Bitten*.

I tend to write random things when gearing up for a new world or winding down from an old one. It's how I say goodbye and process my feelings.

It also gives me closure. It helps me know my happily-ever-after is truly in place. And it grants my mind freedom of creativity.

I don't usually share these with anyone, but I thought you all might want a chance to check in on these characters like I did.

So remember that this is simply meant for enjoyment.

It's not plot heavy.

It's not story heavy.

It's just for **fun**.

And naturally, it's hot.

These are happily-ever-afters, yes? ;)

xx,

Lexi

Once upon a time, vampires and lycans ruled the world.
This is still that time.
Only human rights are on the rise, and vampire mates and
alpha females are considered queens.
The future beyond **Cruelly Bitten** is waiting.
Proceed at your own risk.

CHAPTER ONE

JULIET

WHERE ARE YOU, DARLING? DARIUS'S ACCENTED WORDS warmed our bond, his deep voice a welcome sound in my mind.

In the library, I told him, my gaze on the book in my lap.

Wind stirred around me as Darius phased into the room, his all-black suit impeccable as always. Yet his dark hair held a slight curl to it, the only indication that he'd been moving at impossible speeds through the manor.

His sharp green eyes shone with interest as he took in my reading material, his brow lifting slightly. "The history of Russian?"

I shrugged. "If I'm going to teach linguistics at Darius University, then I need to study some Slavic languages."

His lips curled. "Professor Juliet."

"It was your idea," I reminded him.

"Indeed it was," he agreed, dropping to his knees rather than joining me on the chaise. "Then you can call me *Headmaster Darius*."

"Is that your wish, Sire?" I asked him softly. "To be called *Headmaster Darius* from now on?"

He was the reason the university existed, after all. It'd been his idea, one Jace had supported. While the school primarily focused on trades, there were a few arts programs, including foreign languages. Which I'd expressed an interest in joining.

Darius had felt it was a *brilliant*—his term—idea. "We need more human professors," he'd clarified. "The mortals don't seem all that keen on learning from vampires and lycans."

"Not surprising. It probably reminds them of the Blood Universities or, in my case, the Coventus," I'd told him.

But it was nothing like that. It was a proper university that humans, lycans, and vampires could attend. However, it was geared toward adults.

Other schools had been created for younger humans and lycans—there were no young vampires—to attend.

It was a very different world today, one I didn't fully comprehend yet. But I much preferred it to the one I'd been raised to accept.

"Hmm," Darius hummed now, his palms finding my bare calves beneath my silky robe. While I was free to wear whatever I desired, I still preferred to dress in minimal clothing when at home.

It'd been well over a decade since my time at the Coventus, yet everything continued to feel wrong against my skin.

Perhaps time would cure me of that problem. Perhaps not.

"I do like how that sounds on your lips, Professor Juliet," he murmured, his mouth finding my inner knee. "Even more motivation to let you study. Alas…" His touch slid upward, slightly nudging the book in my lap without knocking it off completely. "I'm famished."

I started to close my text, only for his palm to stop me.

"Oh, no. You can keep studying," he murmured as he spread my legs with his opposite hand. "We'll test your ability to focus." He nibbled my inner thigh, his gaze catching mine. "Read aloud to me while I drink, Professor Juliet. *Teach me.*"

His fangs sank into my skin, causing me to jolt in response.

Every time he bit me, it lit my blood on fire. It didn't matter that we'd done this thousands of times before. He drank and I *reacted*. I was made for this, for *him*, and I wouldn't have it any other way.

Oh, he'd offered to turn me. To make me a vampire. But I preferred our dynamic. I loved the way he craved me for sustenance and sex, the fact that I was the only one he ever desired.

Because he was my world, too.

My Darius.

My vampire.

My headmaster.

He growled into my mind, his irises turning a forest green—the color of arousal. *You're not doing a very good job focusing, darling,* he murmured via our bond. *Do I need to stop?*

"No," I whispered aloud, my stomach clenching. "Don't stop."

Then do your job, he told me. *Read to me.*

I closed my eyes and stole a deep breath as ecstasy warmed my veins. Darius's vampiric kiss always forced me to climax, his rapturous venom an addictive substance that he constantly released via his bite.

He could hold it back.

Yet he never did.

He loved making me come almost as much as I loved pleasing him.

I bit my lip, my training kicking in as I forced myself to ignore the bliss flooding my system and opened my eyes once more.

Then I began to read.

Not that the words made any sense to me.

It was gibberish.

Something about the first Slavic language and Thessaloníki and Greek Macedonia.

By the time I finished the page, I was panting.

"D-darius," I stammered, my heart beating a mile a minute against my rib cage.

"Keep going," he demanded.

"But… but I need…" I shuddered, his tongue a

delicious promise against my thigh. "I need you between my... my thighs."

"I am between your thighs, love," he whispered, biting me again.

My back bowed off the chaise, the book nearly falling to the floor as I scrambled to grab a fistful of his hair.

Keep. Reading. The command echoed in my mind, Darius's voice holding a dominance I couldn't ignore.

He was always like this. Especially in the bedroom. *My Master. My Sire. My Darius.*

Swallowing, I unwove my fingers from his thick strands and shifted my attention to the book. It took considerable discipline to start reading again, my body *burning* from his sensual assault.

A sensual assault that heightened as his palms moved to my hips, his arms now under my robe and the book I had on my lap.

It made it hard to read.

Impossible to focus.

So deliriously *distracting*.

"Please," I begged. "Please, Darius."

"Mmm," he hummed, his fangs leaving my thigh. "Please what, darling? You know how I feel about specifics."

I trembled, his thumbs brushing decadent circles against my hip bones. "Please lick my pussy, Headmaster," I told him, aware of what he wanted to hear.

My Darius craved consent.

And he loved it when I begged him for pleasure.

"I want to come in your mouth," I went on. "Then I want you to fuck me and fill me with your claim. Make me walk around while your seed soaks my thighs."

"Fuck, darling," he whispered, his grip tightening. "I adore it when you tell me what you need." He knocked the book to the floor and pressed his mouth to my sex, his lips unerringly finding my clit.

He didn't lick me.

He *bit* me.

"Darius!" I screamed, my body flying up off the chaise, only for his palm on my lower belly to shove me right back down.

It was intense.

Fast.

Too much.

And... *Ohhh, so good.*

I grabbed his hair again, holding him to me as he released me from his bite, only to clamp down and lick me to completion. His name left my lips on a prayer as he mastered my body with his tongue, his touch exactly what I desired and more.

He slid two fingers into me, not bothering at all with being gentle. Because of course he wouldn't. This was Darius.

Foreplay was an art to him.

But sometimes, he went straight for the heart of it. And it seemed tonight was one of those nights.

My inner walls clenched around him, instantly

craving something thicker. Something *harder*. However, he wasn't done devouring me. A fact he made clear as he growled against my sensitive nub, right before his incisors pierced my skin again.

Another scream escaped me, my body on fire from his ministrations.

I couldn't stop coming.

It was as though my entire purpose of being was to orgasm. Over and over and over again.

Tears flooded my vision.

My throat felt raw.

My lower half *throbbing.*

Embrace it, Darius whispered through my mind. *Embrace every second of it.*

A command.

A wistful sentiment.

A *need*.

I couldn't define that tone of his or the meaning behind it, perhaps because it was a mixture of all of the above.

Darius was complex. He'd always been this way, would always *be* that way. Yet I loved him more than anything.

And I could feel that emotion echoed back to me via our bond.

He didn't care about anyone like he did me. I was his everything. His version of a goddess.

Our decade together hadn't diminished his desires at all, only bolstered them that much more. He could easily understand how his maker, Cam, had stayed with Izzy for over a thousand years. Because Darius fully intended to be with me for even longer.

Forever, his mind told me. *For eternity.*

It was a sentiment we shared.

I wanted to grow with him, to explore more of this new world and find my place within it.

Becoming a professor might be that path. Or maybe I would choose to teach the young.

Regardless, I liked the concept of learning and sharing knowledge, just like Darius did.

He'd taught me so much over the years, and not just in the bedroom.

Yet every experience had seemed to provide something new.

And this one was no different.

"You're going to ride me," Darius said, my robe disappearing as he engaged his vampiric speed to shift our locations around on the chaise.

In a blink, I was straddling him, his cock already free from his pants and poised right at my entrance. I had no idea how he'd done that so quickly, but it instantly stole the air from my lungs.

Air that I immediately inhaled as he impaled me in a single stroke.

His hands were on my hips, guiding me down and up again as I regained my bearings, my mind splintering between action and fantasy. He'd knocked me into an orgasmic stupor, my insides smoldering from his sensual impact.

I grabbed his shoulders to keep my balance, my thighs clamping down around his.

Then I dug my nails into his suit jacket, my eyes finally focusing on his handsome features.

There was a smug grin tugging at his full lips, his arrogance written all over his sculpted jaw. I wanted to dismantle that look. Startle *him* into a rapturous daze.

His eyes seemed to say, *Do your worst, love.*

So I gave him a look right back that said, *I will.*

I leaned in and bit his bottom lip hard enough to bleed, aware that it would jolt him into action. Only, I made him chase my mouth as I tilted my hips into his, driving him that much deeper.

He growled in response, his arm wrapping around my lower back, his opposite palm going to my hair and tangling with my strands.

I smiled and sank my blunt teeth into his neck, desperate for his blood, his healing essence exactly what I needed to clear my mental fog.

Except he bit me right back, returning me to my spiral of ecstasy.

I moaned his name, my breasts pushing against his chest as I rode him—just like he'd said I would. Only it was my pace now, his arm simply a band of support along my spine.

He growled when I bit him again, the sound a reverberation that made it even more difficult to breathe.

Then he angled himself upward, *deep*, causing me to quiver with pleasure.

Come again for me, love, he said into my mind. *Soak my cock for me. Squeeze it. Make me drench you with my seed.*

Tears openly streamed down my face, my body ravaged by his pleasurable assault. Yet I couldn't stop desiring *more*.

His blood healed me while his fangs destroyed me.

It was an intoxicating conundrum that had me falling apart on top of him, my inner walls clenching violently around Darius's throbbing shaft.

He snarled in response, his excitement heightening in our bond as he followed me over the cliff into oblivion, his feral possession leaving me breathless.

And then he was kissing me.

Owning me with his tongue.

Promising me everything with his mouth.

Loving me with his touch.

I shook. Cried. Screamed. *Begged.*

Because the spiral of pleasure wouldn't end.

It drowned me in a sea of darkness, the stars exploding in my wake.

Being with Darius was always like this—all-encompassing madness.

I loved it. Loved him. Loved *life*.

By the time I resurfaced, it was to find myself in the bath with him, his reverent hands roaming over me as he kneaded my stiff muscles.

It was amazing how quickly he could wreck me.

But I wouldn't have it any other way, something I showed by slowly turning to straddle him once more.

He was already hard. Because of course he was. It was Darius. That episode on the chaise had been his version of edging.

He would keep fucking me until it took hours for me to come to.

And I would enjoy every minute of it.

I can study more tomorrow, I told him, my tongue sliding between his lips as I engaged him in a tender kiss.

No, he whispered, his cock sliding into me. *Tomorrow, you'll come with me to the university and help me teach.*

I pulled back to stare at him, our lower halves still intimately connected. "What?"

"It's a class you've already mastered," he murmured, his palm cupping my jaw as he drew a thumb across my lips. "One about history."

My eyes widened. "Human history?"

He nodded. "Jace gave me permission to give a course on it. Not that I actually needed or desired said permission, but he provided it nonetheless."

I wrapped an arm around his neck, my body slowly moving against his below. "I think I'll enjoy your lecture tomorrow."

"Oh, you absolutely will," he promised, his gaze darkening with a deviousness I felt pulsing between our souls. "I bought you a toy to wear for the lecture, one I fully intend to control."

My eyebrows rose. "A toy?"

He grinned. "One that vibrates."

"I…" I wasn't sure what to say. I was both terrified and excited by that prospect.

"You're going to sit in the front row, Professor Juliet. Wear a short skirt. Button-down shirt. And listen while I teach. Then, if you've been a good girl, I'll fuck you on my desk after everyone leaves." His mouth went to my ear. "And then you can scream *Headmaster Darius* for the entire campus to hear."

My legs tensed against him. "Oh." *Oh, yes.* I liked this plan. "I would enjoy that very much, Sire."

"I know," he murmured, his lips hovering against my throat. "It'll be a fantasy for both of us, sweet Juliet." His fangs skimmed my thrumming pulse. "A fantasy that I'm going to make a reality, just like you made the fantasy of having a mate my reality."

I shuddered, his heart in those words.

Darius didn't usually express much sentiment or emotion. He was ancient in so many ways. But with me, he often let his walls down, let me see and feel the affections of his heart.

I loved these moments.

Just as I loved the pleasure that always followed.

Always intense. Always impactful. *Always perfect.*

Make love to me, Darius, I asked him now. *Take me slow. Please.*

Anything for you, my darling, he whispered back into my mind, his mouth moving to mine rather than remaining against my neck. *I love you, Juliet.*

I love you, too, Darius.

CHAPTER TWO
CALINA

"I WANT TO TEACH AT DARIUS UNIVERSITY," I SAID TO Jace as I entered his office. "Humans need medical training. I'm a suitable candidate for such a position."

His dark brows went up, the translucent screen before him displaying Kylan.

"Darius University?" Kylan repeated.

"Yes, it opened earlier this year. It's named after Darius because it's his pet project," Jace informed him. "It's similar to the academic programs Angelique has created in your territory, only it's a more collegiate level, and the lycans, vampires, and humans in my territory are allowed to enroll. Assuming they meet Darius's strict standards."

"I see." Kylan sounded thoughtful. "I would have thought that'd be more appropriate in another decade or so, what with most of the humans of age being too terrified to do anything other than serve, but perhaps it's something we should be looking at sooner rather than later."

"As I said, it's a pet project," Jace repeated. "One that seems to have caught the interest of my little genius."

I stared at him, waiting for him to hang up.

Because yes, it had indeed caught my attention.

I'd given it a lot of thought over the last few months, considering whether or not we could replicate the notion here in Jace City. However, it made more sense to ensure Darius University succeeded first, then create branches throughout Jace Region.

Or perhaps even expand into other places, such as Ivan Region. His territory bordered ours and he was Jace's grand-progeny, so that would make sense for a secondary location.

As part of Lilith's former territory—which had been divided into three different regions several years ago—it was very likely needed there.

You've been busy, Jace murmured into my mind, obviously overhearing all of the ideas roaming through my mind.

I'm always busy, I informed him. *You put me in charge of Jace Medical, which is fine, but I need more staff. And the best way to do that is to train them at a place like Darius University.*

His silver-blue irises glimmered as he replied, *It's* Calina Medical, *little doctor. Not* Jace Medical. *Your failure to remember that has me questioning your cognitive abilities.*

I simply stared at him. *My cognitive abilities are fine, My Prince.*

Those alluring eyes of his narrowed. "I need to see to my *Erosita*, Kylan. Is there anything else you require before I hang up?" Jace asked.

"Hmm, not for now. I'll let Maeve know to expect the tech shipment tonight. Thank you."

Jace nodded, then the screen disappeared.

"We're sending tech to Kylan Region?" I blinked at him. "Why wouldn't he just go to Khalid?" His technology had proved to be superior to everyone else's; why bother trading with anyone else?

"Because it's Kylan. He's very selective when it comes to his friends."

"Yet he adores Ryder." Something I didn't quite understand. The royal was reckless, still refused to play by anyone else's rules, and was absolutely abhorrent when it came to politics.

"As I said, he's selective. And so is Ryder," Jace murmured. "But enough about the other royals in your life, my doctor. Tell me more about this idea of yours to open a medical wing at Darius University."

His possessive choice of *my doctor* didn't escape me. The two words alone were enough to ignite a flurry of butterflies in my lower belly.

Of course, Jace's mere presence alone did that to me.

He's a sensual predator, after all, I thought.

I heard that, he said via our connection as he pushed away from his desk.

It's not a lie, I replied flatly. *It's a fact.*

He arched a brow, his steps sure as he stalked toward me. I lifted a palm to stop him, only it was too late because my hand met his hard abdomen instead. "I came here to talk to you about a medical wing."

"Really? Because it's beginning to feel like you came here to seduce me," he replied, his palm finding my hip as he walked me backward into a wall. "And you call me the *sensual predator.*"

"Says the *sensual predator* trapping me in his office," I returned.

"No trapping required, darling doctor." He pressed a kiss to the edge of my mouth. "You'll stay right there willingly."

I swallowed. "I'm serious, Jace. I want…" I trailed off as his thumb stroked the top of my jeans.

"You want…?" he prompted when I didn't speak again.

"To talk…" I trailed off again, my eyelashes fluttering as his lips traced across my cheekbone to my ear.

"To talk…?" he repeated, his teeth skimming my earlobe.

"About… about…" I cleared my throat, my head falling back into the wall behind me. "Medical school."

"I'm listening," he promised, his lips going to my throat as his thumb continued to tease my lower abdomen. "What about medical school, darling? Are you proposing to go lead the endeavor yourself? Because that's not going to happen."

I frowned, his words helping to chase away some of the sensually induced fog in my mind. "And why not?" I demanded. "I have over a century of experience. I've trained dozens of lab techs and other doctors. I'm more than capable of teaching humans some basic medical knowledge."

And the idea that he didn't think I could achieve that, well, it pissed me off.

I tried to shove him away, irritated now more than turned on.

But he caught my wrists in one hand and easily held them over my head, his vampire prowess one-upping my convoluted mix of genetics.

"Let go of me," I commanded, furious now.

The asshole smiled in response. "Calm down, enchantress. Listen to my mind. Understand my logic."

I glared at him, unsure if I wanted to follow his command. But I did it anyway, mostly because I couldn't fathom a reason as to why he would so swiftly reject my idea. It was practical and absolutely the right...

Hmm, I hummed, the fight draining from my limbs as I found the piece of his thoughts that explained his unexpected response. *Oh.*

Jace had no qualms about me leading the project. Nor did he have any concerns over such an endeavor, save one detail—it would require me to relocate to Darius University.

"You're not leaving me," he murmured. "Further, you can't just abandon Calina Medical. They need your guidance, little genius. However, I think it's a great concept, one we should absolutely continue discussing later."

My brow furrowed. "Later?"

He made an affirmative noise, his silver-blue eyes capturing mine. "Yes, *later*." He popped the button on my jeans, his fingers deftly drawing down the zipper. "A challenge was made, one I'm accepting." His lips went to my ear. "It seems my little genius is in need of a reminder that my sensuality has nothing to do with being a predator and everything to do with being *me*."

I shivered. "I see." I cleared my throat. "Are we setting parameters for this experiment?"

"The only parameter we need is your voice," he murmured as he tugged down my jeans. "Because I'm going to make you scream so hard that you lose it. Start timing, little genius."

The world spun around me before I could respond, my bare ass hitting Jace's desk in the next moment. I yelped, my hands on his shoulders as I tried to right myself, only to fall backward onto his papers in the following instant.

"*Jace*," I hissed, my back arching when he bit my hip bone.

"Too fast, sweet doctor?" he asked, his palms

skimming up my sides as he righted me once more. "Let me fix that."

He gently pulled my sweater up and over my head, leaving me in a bra and a thong before him.

"So pretty," he praised, admiring the blue lace hugging my curves. His fingertips traced my cleavage, his gaze following the motion as he slowly tugged the bra downward to expose my nipples. "*Very* pretty." He leaned down to capture a stiff bud between his teeth, his nibble going straight to the apex between my thighs.

No cheating, I breathed into his mind.

I never cheat, Calina.

Biting is cheating, I clarified as heat spread across my chest. *Vampire venom. Cheating. Yes?*

My words didn't make sense, primarily because he'd sucked my hard peak into his mouth, his tongue taunting my senses. *No venom required,* he murmured back to me. *Now lie there and take it, little doctor. And remember, you did this to yourself.*

He sucked my nipple deep into his mouth before I could reply, one of his hands palming my other breast. Then he switched, abusing my other tip with his tongue and teeth and causing me to squirm on his desk.

"Jace," I whispered, my core throbbing to life.

But he ignored me.

Instead, he kept licking and sucking and nibbling my breasts until the tips were so tender and wet that I could barely think.

He wasn't doing anything to me below, just leaving my center unfilled and untouched, yet I felt like I was close to coming.

It was insanity. No one should be that skilled with breast play. *No one.* And yet Jace was. He was a master of all things pleasurable. A god when it came to delivering orgasms. An expert at edging, too.

And he knew it.

His confidence sang through our bond, that self-assurance a fucking turn-on.

I didn't want him to win, but was this even a game?

No. It was a scientific experiment, one I was absolutely going to benefit from.

He smirked, obviously listening to my analysis. He responded by fisting my hair and pulling me in for a kiss.

His lower half finally met mine with the movement, his cock hard through his silky dress pants and pressing against my soaking wet center. The thong didn't matter. It was a scrap of material that did nothing to hide my need.

A need he caused to burn even hotter as he rubbed against me.

My abused breasts met his dress shirt, the material erotic and sensual against my sensitive tips.

His hand remained in my hair as his opposite one went to my hip, his grip forcing my sex against his as he moved forward, the impact nearly making me orgasm.

He grinned, clearly feeling how pent up and ready I was, not just because I was soaking his trousers but because he could hear it in my mind.

"Ready to scream, doctor?" he asked me softly, his knowing tone a warm welcome to my senses.

Jace didn't give me a second to think, instead pressing against me in just the right way to send me careening over the edge into a cataclysmic climax.

My clit pulsed in response, his dick having nudged it through his pants and my panties. He kept the pressure, drawing out my orgasm and leaving me quivering on his desk.

"Just a sensual predator?" he asked.

"Yes," I told him. "Yes, that."

"Hmm, not nearly hoarse enough," he mused, his fingers tucking into my thong and ripping it from my body in the next breath. "You need at least six more."

My eyebrows rose. "Six?"

"Start counting," he said in reply as he pushed me back down against his desk and settled his mouth between my thighs.

"Jace..." I trailed off as heat blossomed inside me, his mouth sinful and hot and too damn *skilled*.

He didn't need his fangs, just his tongue.

I arched into him, only for his palm to push me right back down.

His opposite hand drifted up my thigh to tease my drenched sex.

An orgasm slammed into me as he inserted two fingers, his touch curling upward and forcing me into a rapturous cycle that seemed to repeat almost as soon as it began.

Count, Calina, he demanded into my head.

O-one, I replied. *I-I think.*

He growled, his tongue massaging my swollen flesh and making me dizzy with intense sensations.

"Jace, I... Jace!" His incisor brushed over my clit, just sharp enough to send a jolt through my being. Then his tongue chased away the pain, sending me spiraling into a dark oblivion.

Where I stayed for a while.

Pulsing over and over again.

Counting.

Losing my mind.

Loving every sensual moment created by Jace's mouth.

By the end of his assault, I was speechless, my throat so raw from screaming that I couldn't speak. Just like he'd promised.

And not once had he bitten me.

It'd all been Jace and his magical touch.

"Still just my vampire prowess?" he taunted.

"No," I exhaled, the word barely audible.

Which only made him smile. "There's our parameter," he mused, standing between my sprawled thighs. "I believe I've made my point."

I nodded as he unfastened his belt. *Yes.*

"How sore is your throat?" he asked, his fingers undoing his button. "Do you want something to swallow? Something warm and soothing?"

My mouth went dry at the thought, my throat instantly working as though I were already drinking from him.

"Think you can kneel for me, sweetheart?" he asked, leaning over me and tracing my jaw with his thumb. "Or did I work you too hard?"

That last bit was a taunt, one that had me forcing myself upright.

His lips twitched, his arrogance on full display.

I'm immortal, I reminded him mentally, as my voice was probably still hoarse, which would have undermined my statement.

I was indeed immortal. I just healed slower.

But I'd healed more than enough to *swallow* for him.

Amusement teased the corners of his mouth as I pushed him back toward the couch in his office. He fell gracefully into the cushions, his arms automatically sprawling along the back as his knees fell naturally apart.

He'd only unfastened the button of his pants, leaving the zipper up.

Rather than fix it, I removed my bra first and tossed it at him. He caught it in midair, his fingers curling into a fist. "I'll be keeping this, darling enchantress."

That's fine. You bought it, I reminded him as I went to my knees.

He chuckled and set the garment aside, then threaded his fingers through my hair. "Impress me," he demanded, fully aware his words would light a fire inside me.

Because I loved it when he challenged me.

Particularly when we both knew I would more than exceed his expectations.

You're not the only one with a sensual prowess, My Prince, I said into his mind, aware that nickname would make him even harder.

He enjoyed it when I called him *My Prince,* even though I typically voiced it with sarcasm. Perhaps that was precisely why he liked it.

Holding his gaze, I drew the zipper down on his pants and freed his impressive length.

No boxers or undergarments. Just pure, hot male.

Licking my lips, I bent to take him into my mouth and groaned as his precum touched my tongue. I swallowed eagerly, telling him without words that he'd been right to offer this as a soothing reward.

I was addicted to his taste.

Addicted to *him.*

And I let him know it by worshipping him with my mouth.

Up and down, taking him as deep as my raw throat allowed.

Massaging him with my tongue.

Fondling his balls.

Humming around the tip before going all the way down again.

Over and over. Sucking. Licking. Even nipping.

All the while, I enjoyed his expression, his eyes

glazing over in a way that told me I owned him in this moment. That I was the one in charge. That I would be the female he loved for eternity. Not just because of my ability to take his cock, but because of the way our minds gelled.

We were equals in so many unique ways. Both master chess players. Two perfect mates who knew exactly how to play with one another.

His grip on my hair tightened, his shaft pulsing against my tongue.

"Swallow for me, sweetheart," Jace growled, his neck straining as he forced himself to watch me, to maintain eye contact as he fell apart.

He wanted to watch me drink from him.

And he wanted me to see his pleasure.

I obliged by swallowing him as far as I could and taking his seed into my throat, all why reveling in the clenching of his jaw and dilation of his pupils.

He cursed then, his resolve to continue holding my gaze becoming increasingly difficult as each rope of cum spurted into my mouth. He was losing control, which made me all the more excited to swallow.

I hummed, my teeth teasing his pulsing cock, and nearly smiled when his growl turned into a groan, his control snapping as he thrust himself impossibly deeper.

Still, I took it. I imbibed every drop, even while my eyes watered from my inability to breathe.

Then I gulped in air as he yanked me up off the ground and into his lap. "Exquisite," he said before capturing my mouth in a bruising kiss. "You're definitely a skilled predator with all sexual prowess, little doctor."

I snorted at that. *Are you saying we need another experiment? One where I prove the skill is all mine and not my immortal genetics?*

Yes, he replied, switching to our mental bond. *Let's start now.*

"I'm pretty sure we've already started," I answered aloud, my voice still raspy but recovering.

"No, that was just me providing some relief for your damaged throat," he returned. "*Now* we can truly begin."

I laughed and shook my head. "You're insatiable."

"Says the female who had over seven orgasms in the last hour." He smiled. "Want to make it eight?"

"Only if you take me upstairs. I'd prefer a bed to your desk. It's more practical and more—"

He phased us from the room before I could finish, my back hitting the mattress in what felt like seconds.

"Comfortable," I said on a breath.

"I assure you it won't remain that way for long," Jace promised me as he started removing his jacket and cuff links. "But I'll be sure to make it pleasurable."

"You always do," I told him as I stretched out on the luxurious comforter. "It's part of your nature."

He growled at that. "Craving another experiment already?"

"With you?" My lips curled. "Always."

"Then get ready to scream again, Calina." His button-down shirt dropped to the floor along with his pants and shoes, leaving him gloriously naked.

I allowed my gaze to run over him, my libido almost immediately on fire once more.

"Prepare yourself, doctor. Because this time, I'm going to bite. And then we'll see which orgasm is more impactful—the one coaxed by my venom or the one given to you by my cock…"

CHAPTER THREE
RAE

I SMILED AS TWO OF MY FAVORITE PEOPLE IN THE world laughed, their joy palpable even through the video screens.

Over a decade of freedom and it still sometimes startled me to see them like this, primarily because we'd survived so long by keeping our emotions in check. But not anymore.

"The last thing I want to do is attend another university," Willow said as she and Silas sobered a bit from their laughing fit. "I get that Darius University is different from what we went through, but it's still a hard pass."

Silas snorted. "Look at you using old human terminology."

"Damien has an impressive movie stash that I'm slowly working my way through," Willow explained.

So does Kylan, I thought, smiling again.

"But in this case, the phrase makes sense," Willow

went on. "I have no interest in returning to university life."

"Well, why would you?" Silas asked her. "You have your own personal trainer—Ryder. We all know what kind of skills he's teaching you." Silas waggled his blond brows, causing Willow to roll her eyes.

"I'm not sure I like that tone," Kylan stated as he joined me on the deck outside. "Especially from a male who is *just a friend*."

I sighed and mimicked Willow's action of rolling her eyes, only I wasn't rolling them at Silas so much as Kylan. "He's teasing Willow."

"Oh," Kylan murmured, his expression thoughtful. "Well, by all means, proceed, wolf. And, Willow, do let me know when Ryder heads into Clemente Clan next. I should enjoy watching his next interaction with young Silas."

"It won't be all that eventful," Ryder drawled as he suddenly appeared on the screen. From the image, it seemed he'd been lying in Willow's lap this entire time, perhaps using her thigh as a pillow.

My friend's cheeks tinged pink as though embarrassed by her secret being discovered.

"Unlike you, I don't feel threatened all that easily," Ryder added, causing Kylan to arch a brow.

"Who says I feel threatened?" Kylan demanded.

Ryder snorted. "Your reaction to Silas speaks volumes. He's a mated wolf. Edon would have his balls if he so much as sniffed the wrong way."

Silas scoffed at that.

Willow just shook her head.

And Kylan, well, he simply stared at the screen with a bored expression.

After a beat, he said, "As always, it's been a delight talking with you, Ryder. Unfortunately, Raelyn and I need to go now."

He reached forward to end the call before I had a chance to say anything, causing my eyebrows to lift. "We were in the middle of a conversation about Darius University."

"All the more reason to complete the call," he replied as he picked a snowflake out of my hair. "What a dull conversation."

"It wasn't dull at all. We were discussing the various programs, then that turned into Willow saying how weird it must be to attend, which led us to visualizing it…" I trailed off and shrugged, aware that the conversation wasn't all that important. "We were just bonding about what it must be like compared to what we know."

The conversation would probably have been a sad one among others with our backgrounds, but we were able to find humor in the comparison. Mostly in terms of how different the classes likely were, as well as the university wardrobe.

"Do you want to attend?" Kylan asked me, his tone serious.

I blinked at him, then heaved a small laugh. "Like you'd ever allow that."

His brow came down, suggesting that had been

the wrong answer. "Raelyn, I would let you do whatever you desire. If you don't know that by now, then I'm not sure what to do to convince you."

I grabbed his sweater-clad arm before he could leave.

"That's not what I meant." I searched his gaze, my connection to his thoughts making me realize that I'd hurt him with my words. "I meant that you wouldn't let me leave Kylan Region to reside at Darius University. You'd hate for me to leave. And I would hate it, too. I also don't want to go, so it's a moot point."

He studied me for a long moment, his dark eyes scrutinizing mine. "Are you sure you don't want to go, Raelyn?" he asked after a beat, his mind clearly in tune with mine. "Because I don't think you would even be discussing it if a small part of you wasn't intrigued."

I swallowed, considering his words. "I'm not sure," I admitted. "I don't even know what I would want to study."

"That used to be the beauty of college for humans," he murmured, his palm caressing my cheek. "It was a place for mortals to go and discover their passions, to determine their paths in life." He grabbed my hip with his opposite hand, his body aligning with mine against the porch railing. "Perhaps it's something to think about."

"Or maybe we should consider opening a university here, too," I suggested to him. "We already have schools similar to those in Jace Region, so why not add our own higher-education facility?"

"Is that something you'd like?"

"Maybe. It's not something I would have even imagined, but ever since you told me about your conversation with Jace, I can't stop thinking about what it must be like." Which was why I'd mentioned it to Willow and Silas.

"Then it's something we'll continue to discuss and see what we can develop," Kylan told me, his thumb drawing a line over my bottom lip. "I would give you anything you desire, Raelyn. Always."

"Always?" I asked slowly, my eyebrow inching upward. Because I would very much enjoy making him prove that.

Kylan was domineering and in charge in every way.

I loved that about him.

But sometimes it was fun to push his buttons and determine the limits of his patience.

His lips slowly curved upward, no doubt following the trajectory of my thoughts. "What boundary would you like to test today, little lamb?"

"Hmm." My gaze roamed over him, his handsome state reminiscent of a painting.

His jawline and cheekbones were so perfectly crafted that they almost didn't appear real.

His eyes were an alluring shade of obsidian.

His thick, dark hair was stylishly tousled, not a strand out of place.

And his body… *Mmm, chiseled perfection in a suit.*

But it was his tie that captured my interest most.

Because it was silk.

Which gave me an idea.

"Race you upstairs," I told him, phasing into the house and up the stairs before I finished speaking.

Kylan's growl reverberated in my mind, the sound growing in intensity when he met me in our closet. "A fair race requires an even start."

I bent to grab what I wanted, then stood and blinked at him. "Why would you need an even start? You're, like, a bazillion years old. I'm a baby vampire in comparison."

He narrowed his gaze. "A baby vampire who magically inherited my abilities."

"That's not *my* fault," I told him, my palm pressing to my heart and revealing the silky ropes in my hand.

Of course, he already knew what I'd picked up. It was his box I'd been rummaging through, after all. "And what do you plan to do with those?" he asked, shifting topics to a more sensual one.

"Tie you up," I answered honestly.

He arched a brow. "I'm usually the one who does the tying, Raelyn."

"Yes, and today, the student becomes the master." There was a pun in there somewhere. "I'm going to need you to take off your clothes."

That caused both his eyebrows to lift. "Raelyn…"

"You said you'd give me anything I desire. Right now, that's you, naked, and completely at my mercy."

He stared at me.

And I stared back.

After a few moments' pause, he sighed and unbuttoned his jacket. I watched as he hung it up, then admired the show as he unfastened his cuff links and set them meticulously on the top of his closet dresser.

His tie was next, followed by his dress shirt and undershirt, only he neatly folded those into the laundry basket in the corner.

And finally his pants and socks joined the pile, leaving him gloriously naked and very aroused.

He might prefer to be in charge, but he was certainly intrigued by what I had planned.

"Where to, *Mistress*?" he taunted.

I smiled. "The bedroom, naturally."

He gave me a look that said I'd pay for my sarcasm later, but dutifully trailed after me as I led the way toward our bed. Only, I didn't tell him to get on the mattress. Instead, I gestured to a chair in the seating area.

A chair we both knew well.

Except I was usually the one who sat there while he played with the rope—which was an art he'd introduced me to a few years ago.

An art I very much enjoyed.

But I wanted to tease him now, see how far he would bend beneath my control.

Kylan moved the chair into the bedroom and set it right by the floor-to-ceiling windows, just like he normally would for me. Then he sat without a word and clasped his hands behind his back.

I slowly walked up behind him, evaluating how to proceed.

He usually let me feel the ribbons first, familiarizing the texture with my skin. So I did that by gently brushing the silk against his neck and then down one arm before running it up the other.

Goose bumps pebbled along his flesh, his mind telling me he was proud of me for the slow introduction.

Never rush it, he was thinking. *Good. Very good.*

I let some of the ribbon unfold over his shoulder, leaving it there as I trailed the silky strand across his sculpted chest.

His eyes held mine, his expression heated.

It was different from how we usually did this, when I submitted completely. But I'd give him this show of dominance, primarily because it made me want to squirm beneath his perusal.

He was evaluating me.

Grading my knowledge.

Determining how well I'd paid attention to his previous ministrations.

I swallowed, his study of me leaving me warm all over. Mainly because he was truly interested in how much I'd learned from him.

It made me want to please him.

To prove that I paid attention.

That I *knew* him and his motions and his wants and his needs.

I boldly held his stare as I ran the silky ribbon down his sternum to his rippled abdomen, then lower to whisper across his hard shaft.

His muscles flexed in response, his athletic thighs drawing my gaze downward with interest. *So strong and beautiful,* I thought, loving his masculine form.

If anyone should have been a shifter, it was Kylan. He possessed the grace of an apex predator and the sleekness of a wolf.

Yet he was a vampire.

And not just any vampire, but a vampire *royal.*

One I'd bitten years ago.

One I wanted to bite again now.

Leaning forward, I caught his lower lip between my teeth and gave in to the impulse to draw blood.

He growled again, the sound a rumble-like purr to my senses.

Then I straddled him on the chair and kissed him, my need to be near him taking over my every instinct. He returned my embrace, his tongue dueling mine for domination.

And when that wasn't good enough, he grabbed my nape and truly devoured me.

I lost track of time, too caught up in his expert mouth and his decadent flavor. I couldn't remember the last time I'd fed. It wasn't really necessary, as we tended to add blood to our food.

But Kylan's essence made me feel famished, like I hadn't eaten in years.

Or maybe it was just his addictive kiss.

Regardless, I allowed myself to fall deeper into his sensual trap, my mouth his to claim. My tongue his to master. My body his to explore.

His hands drifted along my sides, my sweater seeming to disappear in a blink.

Then my jeans magically followed, his palms guiding me as though I were his to control. I was only vaguely aware that we were even standing now, my mind utterly consumed by Kylan's seductive prowess.

He chuckled against my mouth, his tongue taunting my lips. "I should tie you up just to teach you a lesson."

"Hmm?" I hummed, confused by his words.

"But I'm feeling too desirous for that right now." He kissed a path to my ear. "Rope play requires time and patience, and while we have ample amounts of the former, I'm sorely lacking the latter."

He tugged me toward the bed, his strong body instantly settling over mine as he pressed me into the mattress.

"You were doing so well until you let me distract you," he murmured, his lips brushing mine. "Now I'm going to accept my reward."

"Reward?"

"Mmm, yes." He kissed the edge of my mouth. "My reward for giving you what you wanted—control. Now I'm taking it back."

His cock slid home inside me in a single thrust, the unexpected impact stealing the breath from my lungs.

I hadn't even felt him move; he was just suddenly *there*.

"Wrap those beautiful legs around me, Raelyn," he demanded. "I want to feel you clamp down around me while I fuck you."

I shuddered, his words an aphrodisiac to my senses.

Every time.

No matter how often he touched me or spoke to me.

I *always* reacted this way to him.

My thighs squeezed his hips as I locked my ankles against his lower back, the action forcing him even deeper.

"Such a good girl," he praised, his shaft throbbing inside me. "Now grab my shoulders."

I did.

"Beautiful," he marveled, his compliment making me all warm and content beneath them.

Then he chased away that contentment with his savage strokes, driving me to a brand-new plane of existence. A plane adorned in heat and sensation. Somewhere I could lose myself entirely and let him tell me how to feel, how to think, how to move. Like a break from reality.

A submissive frame of mind.

I'd been here countless times before, but each

experience was somehow more impactful than the last. And this was no different.

Kylan knew exactly what I needed. How I needed it. Where I needed it. Everything.

I panted beneath him, my nails digging into his shoulders as he ravaged me to completion. Not just with his cock, but with his mouth, too.

And his hands.

Oh, his hands...

They were everywhere.

On my breasts.

My sides.

His thumb stroking my clit.

Cradling my face.

Grabbing my throat.

It was a whirlwind of *Kylan*. So intense. So addicting. So *breathtaking*.

He was everything I desired and more.

And I felt that same devotion echoed back at me through our bond.

However, that didn't stop him from catching my face between his hands and saying, "I love you, Raelyn. I love you more than anything else in this universe. And I mean it—I'll do anything for you. Give you everything. Simply name it and it's yours."

"I just want you," I breathed, arching into him. "Always you."

"You have me."

"Then I'm the luckiest woman alive," I told him,

my body shaking from the onslaught of pleasure rippling through my being. "Fuck me, Kylan."

He grinned. "I am fucking you, sweetheart." He grasped my hips in the next instant, his dark eyes glittering with intent. "But I'm happy to fuck you harder."

I arched into him. "*Yes…*"

"There's just one thing," he said, his mouth at my ear again. "You might be the luckiest woman alive, but I'm the luckiest vampire alive. Because I have you. And I fully intend to cherish you for eternity, my love. Now come around my cock so I can join you in oblivion."

He nibbled my earlobe, his words making me burn.

"Then I'm going to tie you to that chair, spread your legs, and watch as my cum drips from your sweet cunt," he went on. "Maybe I'll push it back inside you. Or maybe I'll feed it to you."

My insides clenched around him, my orgasm mounting to the point of near pain.

He growled, adding, "Or maybe I'll just keep filling you up while you're helpless and bound."

Fuck. I was panting. "*Kylan.*"

"Now, Raelyn," he said, knowing I needed his command. "Come right fucking now."

Everything inside me burst beneath a shock wave of pure ecstasy, my limbs shaking from the release. Tears clouded my vision.

And then Kylan was coming, too, his hot seed coating my insides just like he'd promised.

By the time we both finished, I was a mess of sensation.

But I could hear in his mind that he'd meant every word he'd said.

So when he carried me over to the chair, I wasn't surprised. I simply submitted. I let him seduce me with the ribbon. Gave in to his touch. And relished the way his eyes felt on my skin.

He didn't need to touch me for me to sense him. The bond heightened all that.

I could feel his yearning through our link.

See how he saw me via his mind.

Hear his dark cravings as well as his gentle whispers of praise.

It was intoxicatingly beautiful.

My own perfect version of a happily-ever-after.

Something I'd once thought was impossible in this world.

Kylan had changed everything.

And I'd spend eternity loving every moment with him.

Just as I knew he'd spend eternity loving every moment with me.

"Deep breaths, Raelyn," he whispered now. "I'm about to fuck you again, just like this…"

CHAPTER FOUR
WILLOW

The hairs danced along my arms, my instincts firing in every direction.

He's coming, I thought with a shiver. *The question is, from where?*

This was one of Ryder's favorite games—survivor and hunter, whereby I was the survivor and he was the hunter.

Apparently, it used to be called *hide-and-seek*, something I'd learned from watching one of Damien's old movies. Except Ryder's version of it was a lot more… *violent.*

Swallowing, I checked my gun, ensuring the safety was off.

Ryder could move impossibly fast, making every millisecond count.

He's close, my wolf seemed to think. *Very close…*

I could smell him, that minty aftershave of his a dead giveaway to my enhanced senses. Although, I was perpetually doused in his natural cologne, making it difficult to know how close he actually was.

He would be too silent to hear, his footsteps nonexistent.

And he would be too skilled to slip up.

Which made this game dangerous. He was an apex predator, and while he'd taught me a lot of his tricks, he possessed thousands of years of experience and I possessed a handful of decades.

Not all that fair as far as abilities were concerned, but that was entirely the point—Ryder wanted me to be prepared for every potential scenario.

And that included facing ancient vampires.

The world around us was constantly changing, the political minefield one that shifted daily, thus making it imperative for me to be prepared for anything and everything.

Especially as a hybrid.

The lycans hadn't forgiven vampire kind for what they'd done, and while they weren't actively seeking retribution, there were whispers of discontent— whispers that my best friend Silas had told us about.

Clemente Clan wasn't invited to partake in lycan meetings, mostly because Edon refused to pick a side between vampires and lycans. There were other alphas who agreed with Edon's stance as well, leaving their territories open to negotiations with all the supernaturals of the world.

But some clans were very specific about only trading amongst lycan kind.

It all worked for the moment, everyone existing within their own boundaries and beneath their own laws. However, there was no harm in preparing for potential chaos.

Hence, Ryder's favorite pastime of survivor and hunter.

I hunkered down in the little alcove I'd found about two miles away from our cabin, the hairs along my arms still dancing.

Where are you? I wondered, scanning the lush greenery, my nose twitching.

There were so many alluring scents out here with all the blooming flowers and fresh flowing water. Living just outside of Ryder City certainly had its benefits.

Damien maintained the tower in the region's capital, where he managed most of the politics on Ryder's behalf. Fortunately, Damien wasn't alone. He'd turned Tracey into a vampire almost a decade ago and had given her Benita's old role as tower manager. It seemed appropriate after everything Tracey had gone through.

Meanwhile, Ryder and I resided on the outskirts of a nearby jungle.

It was all overgrown with wild animals, plant life, and beautiful colors.

And it provided the perfect playground for Ryder's games.

Deep breaths, I told myself, my ears listening for any alteration of sound. A startled bird. The crunching of a branch. Anything that could tell me Ryder's location.

But as always, my vampire mate was too quiet for my senses.

My ears and nose were my best detectives, my aim my best defense.

I held the gun loose at my side, waiting, watching, *searching*.

Only to jump when my wrist buzzed with an incoming message, one that had me holding my breath as I anticipated Ryder's reaction.

He'd chastise me for not fully silencing my watch, then sensually punish me for failing this mission.

Part of me wanted to be caught for that very reason.

However, the competitor in me needed to be ready to *fight*.

Except he never pounced. There was no movement at all other than the soft flutter of wings and the occasional breeze. *Maybe he's not as close as I originally thought,* I told myself, glancing down at my watch to see if it was Ryder who had messaged me.

I need to cancel our call later today, and I'm going to be out of touch for a while, the text read. *Luna's going into heat.*

My eyebrows went up, the concept hitting me square in the gut.

Lycan heat.

Fortunately, that wasn't something I'd had to experience, likely because my vampire side overrode—

My back hit the earth in a whoosh, causing the air to escape my lungs on a gasp-like scream.

Ryder simply sighed as he settled on top of me. My wrists were trapped beneath one of his palms over my head, and my gun was nowhere in sight.

Shit.

"What has you so distracted, pet?" he asked conversationally, his thumb already pulling up the message from Silas. He hummed as he read it, his black eyes glittering like hard diamonds. "Ah, I see. You're fantasizing about a lycan rut."

"No," I breathed, squirming now that I'd been caught. Which, of course, was several seconds too late. But that didn't mean I'd just lie here and accept fate. "I was thinking that I'm glad I don't go through that." I muttered the words through my teeth, my body straining beneath him in a futile effort to dislodge him.

"Hmm." He was still staring at the message, completely unfazed by me trying to shove him off of me. "Maybe I'm the one fantasizing about a lycan rut, then."

I went still. "*What?*"

"Well, more specifically, about a certain hybrid with lycan genetics and what it might be like if she went into heat." His gaze finally met mine, his pupils pulsating. "I would fuck you for days."

"You already do that."

"Indeed I do," he conceded. "Maybe you should

go into a play heat right now, you know, since it's already on your mind."

I gave him a look. "You mean since it's on *your* mind."

"That, too." He nuzzled my neck, his fangs skimming my pulse. "Mmm, but I would love for you to crawl across the ground. Naked. Dripping wet between your thighs. Begging me to fuck you. Take you. *Possess* you."

I nearly pointed out that we'd done things like that before.

But I was too caught up in his words to fathom an appropriate response. Primarily because I liked the image they painted in my head.

"Yes, let's start now," he decided aloud, rolling off of me. "Strip and run, pet. I want to chase you."

I blinked up at him. "What?" That hadn't been what he'd described. Not entirely, anyway.

He stared down at me, impatience written in the arch of his eyebrow. "You're that distracted that I need to repeat myself?" He folded his arms. "I'm disappointed, pet."

Rolling my eyes, I jumped to my feet and started looking for my gun.

"Willow."

I ignored him, still searching. Because I *really* wanted to shoot him.

A sharp blade suddenly met my neck, forcing me to freeze as his hot, muscular chest met my back. "*Strip*," he demanded. "Now."

My heart skipped a beat.

The predator at my back wasn't known for his leniency, and I could feel the tension coiling in his hard form.

We didn't need a traditional bond to *hear* each other. Our bodies did all the speaking for us. And right now, his was saying, *I'm the hunter and you're the prey. Obey or pay the consequences.*

Shivering, I started with my boots and then my jeans, all the while feeling that lethal edge against my throat. When I reached my tank top, I paused.

Ryder didn't react.

Which meant he wanted me to work around his blade as he refused to move an inch.

I dragged the straps along my arms, then pulled the cotton material down over my hips to shimmy out of it like I'd done with my pants.

It wasn't an easy task. But that was Ryder's way. He loved accepting challenges almost as much as giving them.

When I was fully naked, I simply leaned back into him, telling him without words that I was comfortable with his dominant position at my back.

He placed a kiss on my neck in response, his blade still resting against my throat. Then his lips went to my ear as he whispered a single word, one that sent a chill down my spine. "*Run.*"

The dagger disappeared, but his body heat remained.

We were embarking on a new game now, this one

focusing on me being the prey and him being the predator.

I didn't run; I phased, covering a mile of forest in a blink.

Because I knew this land well. Ryder and I had been playing in it for nearly a decade.

Unfortunately, that meant he knew this land, too.

I teleported down the hill toward a water spring, wanting to rid the air of my scent. Only, a devious thought occurred to me as I reached it. *What if I hid instead?*

Normally, I would make him chase me all over the forest for the scant minutes it would take for him to catch me.

I only ever hid when we were in survivor and hunter mode. But Ryder had already caught his prey, so now he was just playing with his prize.

But maybe I want to play, too, I thought, phasing behind a waterfall. The thick flow hid my view of the woods, but that meant I was concealed as well.

And the waist-deep water in here allowed me to mask my natural perfume, too.

I sank down to my neck and started backward toward the rocky surface behind me.

Except the item I came up against wasn't rocky at all. It was sturdy. Hot. And *masculine.*

My heart jumped into my throat as I shot upward, only to be caught up in bands of steel. "If you wanted to get wet, pet, you should have just told me," Ryder murmured against my ear.

"*Fuck*," I breathed, my pulse rocketing upward in full force. *How the hell does he* do *that?* I marveled, furious that I hadn't even *heard* him, let alone *felt* him. It was like he'd magically appeared right behind me before I'd even gone behind the waterfall.

"That, too," he murmured, his nose nuzzling my neck. "Mmm, definitely that, too."

He spun me toward him, his dark eyes appearing sinister in the low lighting of our cave. I swallowed, both aroused by and terrified of that look.

His full lips curled into a taunting grin. "You're very distracted today, Willow." He drew his nose along my cheek as he softly added, "Or maybe you just wanted to be captured and fucked against the rocks, hmm?"

"I…" I had nothing to say to that. No defense. No excuse. No argument. Just… a sigh. Primarily because he'd slid one sturdy thigh between my legs. His touch hypnotized me, his very presence a *distraction*.

"I…?" he prompted. "I what, pet? *Speak.*"

My jaw clenched, my gaze narrowing. I had no intention of fulfilling *that* command.

Which, naturally, he knew because amusement shone in his dark depths. "You're not going to tell me what you want?" he asked, his tone low, silky, and far too smooth. "You want me to just take what I want instead, little warrior?"

His palms roamed over my bare skin while he spoke, his pupils dilating in a way that told me he was hungry.

If I didn't voice my needs, he'd translate that as me having no limits in mind.

Which meant he could take whatever he wanted, however he wanted it.

"Be sure, sweet pet," he murmured softly, his thumb drawing a circle against my hip bone as his palm slid up to my nape. "I'm in a biting mood." He leaned down to demonstrate against my lower lip, his fangs sharp and deadly and easily drawing blood. "I will fuck you up against that rock wall, and you will bleed for me."

"Good thing I'm immortal, then," I said back to him, not only accepting his challenge but also delivering one of my own.

If he wanted to be rough, I could take it.

And more, I'd *like* it.

He growled, the feral sound vibrating my chest as he drew me closer. "Good choice, *mate*."

His mouth captured mine, his tongue unrelenting. There was no chance to say anything else. No moment to prepare. Just Ryder taking exactly what he wanted—*me*.

I melted into him, letting him lead while reveling in his knowing touch. He would be harsh. Cruel, even. But the end result would be worth the pain. It always was.

His palm squeezed my nape, his mouth hot against mine. "Unfasten my pants and pull out my cock."

I knew better than to argue with him in this state, but I couldn't help taunting him a little.

Rather than unfasten his pants, I forced my nails to transition into claws and ripped his jeans before tugging them down to his thighs. My hand quickly shifted back to normal before I grabbed his shaft, his resulting hiss a violent vow against my lips.

"Oh, you really are the perfect mate," he said, his grip hardening around my nape. "Now turn around and brace against the rocks."

I nipped at his mouth before obeying, earning a growl in my wake.

The sound of rustling clothes tickled my ears as Ryder finished undressing, the water shifting around us with his movements. I had no doubt he could have somehow done that without making a sound or even a ripple, which told me he was creating waves on purpose.

He wanted me to feel him.

To know what he was doing.

To mentally prepare for whatever he had planned.

To draw out the moment and increase my anticipation.

Minutes passed, that sense of expectation growing. He wanted me to pant for him. To fear him. To want him. To fall apart for him.

This was his version of foreplay.

Watching. Waiting. *Admiring*.

I could feel his eyes on me, taking in every exposed curve.

He was like a predator evaluating a meal.

Goose bumps danced along my damp skin, my neck prickling with awareness. Ryder was so silent and still—*a beast waiting to pounce.*

My thighs tensed, my insides burning with growing *need.* He wasn't even touching me, and I was on fire for him. Always.

Fuck, I nearly whispered aloud, my body inflamed in the best way. I loved it when he did this, how he toyed with my mindset, edged my pleasure, and—

I jolted as his lips caressed the base of my spine, his touch so sudden that my toes curled. His name left my tongue, my back automatically arching toward him. But he only allowed me to feel his mouth, his kisses whisper-soft as he trailed them upward to my nape.

"Mate," he growled near my ear, his lower half pressing against mine.

His cock was so thick and hard, his heat an invitation I longed to accept. "Mate," I echoed back to him, the word escaping me on a moan that I felt vibrate through my entire being.

He nipped my neck in response, his fangs sharp against my skin. "I wanted to take your ass," he told me darkly. "But I'm suddenly craving something else."

The world spun as he yanked me around to face him, his mouth crashing down on mine with a ferocity I craved. His tongue mastered me, but I refused to fully submit, my nails biting into his shoulders as I fiercely clung to him.

I was only vaguely aware of him phasing us deeper into the cave, the secret alcove entirely hidden by the waterfall. We'd played in here before, the slippery rocks making for some interesting positions. One of which he assumed now as he leaned back against a slanted surface and pulled me onto him, his cock nudging at my entrance.

"Ride me, mate." He punctuated his demand by thrusting up into me.

My back bowed as pleasure hummed along my spine.

Denying his command wouldn't have been possible even if I'd wanted to defy him.

My body knew his, my instincts tied to Ryder in every way. I didn't even care that the rocks bit into my knees. Instead, I welcomed the pain, just as I reveled in the ecstasy his strokes evoked below.

He grabbed my hips as he drove up into me, his touch taking control of my pace as he told me without words what he wanted.

I bit his tongue, desiring his blood.

He responded in kind, our kiss turning into a violent embrace between our mouths.

He rumbled in approval. I moaned. Our bodies *fucked*.

It was animalistic. Fierce. Utterly feral. And so very us.

I wrapped my arms around his neck, my breasts pushing up against his chest as we continued our carnal dance. His movements turned savage, his grip bruising.

He phased us again, this time pressing me up against the rocky cave wall. I barely felt it, his sensual assault masking the abrasive texture digging into my back.

All I wanted was more.

More Ryder.

More blood.

More *thrusts*.

He gave me everything, his body worshipping mine on a primal level.

"I need you to come for me, pet," he snarled against my mouth. "Squeeze me with that hot, wet cunt. Help me take the edge off so I can fuck you for hours."

I shuddered, his words setting my veins on fire.

Because he meant them.

He fully intended to fuck me all night, and I had no qualms about it. Especially if he kept phasing us around like this.

My thighs tensed around him as he slammed into me, his forceful movements demanding that I adhere to his order—*to come*.

I panted, an inferno building between my legs.

It was always like this—intense, all-encompassing, *mind-blowing*.

Yet it startled me each time.

It was like I could never grow used to this rapturous plane of existence. Nor did I want to. I loved how this felt, that feeling like I was about to either die or fly. It made my heart race, caused my breathing to falter, and enraptured my mind.

Ryder was everywhere.

Kissing me.

Fucking me.

Taking me.

I loved him more than anything. Loved *this*. And I told him that with my movements.

"*Now*, Willow," he breathed against my ear, his mouth falling to my neck.

I trembled, anticipating his bite.

And fell over the cliff right before his fangs entered my skin.

"*Ryder!*" I screamed, my climax intensified by his venom and causing my thoughts to blank entirely.

Darkness engulfed me.

Inky bliss.

That beautiful plane of existence where I just luxuriated in aftershocks of immense gratification.

Ryder's chest vibrated against mine, the only indication that he'd fallen over that addictive edge with me. He was still drinking from my vein, his cock pulsing deep inside me.

Driving me onward.

Forcing me to remain in this whirlpool of euphoria.

It went on.

And on.

And *on*.

Until I lost touch with reality.

Only to wake with my head against a soft pillow and Ryder looming over me with a self-satisfied grin on his too-handsome face. "Ready, mate?"

I blinked at him, my body still sore from everything he'd done to me.

Time was a meaningless concept.

I could have been out for minutes or hours. Probably somewhere in between because I was no longer wet, my body seeming to have been towel-dried by the predator hovering above me.

He'd obviously phased us back to our room.

My lips curled as he studied me, his obsidian eyes glittering with dark intent.

"I'm ready," I whispered to him.

"Good." He pressed his hardness against my soft heat. "Now hold on to the headboard, pet. And remember your safe word. It's going to be a long night..."

CHAPTER FIVE
LUNA

My paws pounded against the earth, my wolf sprinting across the land at full strength.

We wouldn't be able to maintain this speed for long, especially with my insides going up in flames. But we had to try. To test. To *fight*.

A whine caught in my throat as my belly clenched, my heat burning a wanton path through my veins.

Not yet, I told my treacherous hormones. *Make them work for it.*

Oh, we're going to make you *work for it, little mate*, Edon taunted into my mind. *All fucking week.*

I nearly tripped in response to that sensuous threat, but somehow my animal maintained control and kept us on our paws.

This game was unlike any we'd ever played. Primarily because there was a reward at the end that we all craved—*a pup.*

My insides turned to mush at the thought, my

body more than ready to give my mates what they desired. But I had to push them, to make them *earn* this. It was all instinct, my wolf demanding her beasts force her to submit.

Which wasn't an easy feat, considering my animal and I were all alpha female.

However, if anyone could make me heel, it would be Edon and Silas.

We can smell you, little moon, Silas murmured into my mind. *Your arousal is like a fucking beacon.*

Mmm, a beacon I can't wait to lick and suck until you're begging for our cocks, Edon echoed.

I swallowed, my steps nearly faltering once more.

These males didn't play fair.

You're stronger than this, I told myself. *Keep. Going.*

Edon's amusement taunted my steps, his self-assurance an irritation and a turn-on.

Silas was less amused but equally as determined.

Ever since we'd decided my next heat would be *the one*, my mates had become even more attentive and competitive. The pack expected Edon to be the one to produce an heir, but he and Silas had other plans. They wanted to battle it out.

By fucking me. At the same time.

I shivered, anticipation racing down my spine.

My mind was slowly succumbing to need, my heat taking me to that place where there was only one desire in life—*to procreate.*

Usually, Edon and Silas took turns satisfying me during my heat in a safe manner, the three of us having decided to wait until the time was right to make a baby.

But now that Clemente Clan was firmly under our rule—and thriving because of it—we felt ready to bring a life into the world.

Only, none of us wanted to choose who the father would be.

"It doesn't matter," Edon had said. "Silas and I will both be his or her father, just as Luna will be the mother."

Most alphas would never say something like that, their need to create an heir embedded in their genetic makeup.

But Edon had meant every word. Even if Silas sired the baby, Edon would consider it his, and vice versa.

Which only made this all the more fun.

Because both males had decided this would be a new experience—sharing me in a way they never had before.

Oh, I was used to being between them in bed. However, they had something different in mind for today. Something *exciting*.

So exciting that I nearly stopped running to shift, my need to roll over and wait threatening to overtake my resolve.

No, no. Run. Chase. Hide. Fight. The words were broken in my thoughts, but my wolf understood the assignment, our paws still pounding over the ground. *Faster. Harder. More…*

All things I plan to make you say the moment I have you on your back, little mate, Edon said into my mind. *All while I force you to come over and over again.*

Silas hummed in agreement, the sound so loud it almost felt like he was beside me.

I could smell them now, their scents combining into an alluring cologne. *A refreshing new day in a decadently dark forest,* I marveled, inhaling deeply. *Yes, please.*

Both my mates growled back at me, the sound not just in my mind but also reverberating around me.

They're here, I told my wolf.

But she already knew. Her excitement at being caught caused her to leap forward into the underbrush, our tail high and waving at the males as though to say, *Come and get me.*

The wolves behind me rumbled in anticipation, their need to rut nearly suffocating my thoughts. They were going to destroy me in the best way.

I bounded off of a rock into the water, my animal splashing along to the other side in a playful way that normally would have made me roll my eyes. However, right now, we were on the same wavelength. We wanted to tempt our mates.

Silas attempted to tackle us first, but my wolf was smaller and faster and jumped out of the way at just the precise moment.

Only to find ourselves suddenly trapped under Edon.

He snarled, victory radiating off of his much larger form.

You played me, I realized, accusing both of my mates of tricking me into this direction.

We won you, Edon corrected, his muzzle going to my throat as he gently nipped at me. *Shift back, little mate. Let us have you.*

He could technically force me to shift with a growl, but I appreciated him for not making me submit in that way. It showed respect, something I rewarded by adhering to his request.

His wolf rumbled in approval as I turned into a human beneath him, my bare skin pebbling with goose bumps from both his presence above me and the chilly water beneath me. It was an intoxicating combination that left me breathless.

He lowered his snout to my neck again, his teeth parting around my tender throat in a way that expressed complete and utter domination.

I remained absolutely still, submitting to his beast.

Then Silas nudged him out of the way to give my tender skin a firm lick that turned into a sweet kiss as he shifted beside me.

Edon was the last to assume his human form, his eyes resembling twin black flames. "Move her to the grass," he demanded, his words for Silas.

My blond-haired mate lifted me into his arms, his mouth caressing my cheek as he carried me out of the creek and over to a soft bed of grass nearby. The hairs along my arms danced in response, my insides turning to molten need at feeling the warmth of my mates.

I was close to losing myself to my heat.

Once that happened, I'd be out of my mind for days, trapped in a rapturous state of arousal while my males rutted me over and over again.

Silas kissed me, his thoughts rivaling my own as he came over me, his hips pressing into mine.

Edon said something I didn't quite hear. Whatever it was, it made Silas murmur in agreement right before his tongue slid into my mouth.

I lost track of time and space as he devoured me, his touch knowing. His lips addicting. His hot form exactly what I craved.

He was coaxing me into submitting in an entirely different way, his body telling me I belonged to him through sensation alone.

I yielded once more, my legs parting around his, my bare center eagerly embracing his arousal. Only, he didn't slide into me. Instead, he simply ran his palms up and down my sides, the tip of his cock resting right against my clit.

Silas, I hissed, arching into him.

Luna, he returned, nipping at my bottom lip. "Edon wants you to beg," he whispered against my mouth. "Want me to help that along, little moon?"

I squirmed beneath him. "I want you to fuck me."

"That's not begging," Edon murmured. "Maybe you should start preparing her for us, Enforcer. Fuck her with your tongue. But don't let her come."

Silas hummed again, smiling. "Happily, Alpha." He nibbled my lower lip once more before kissing a path down my neck and lower to my breasts. "Her tits need your mouth, Edon."

"Mmm, do they?" he murmured, his dark eyes coming into view as he knelt beside me. "Teeth or tongue?"

Both, I thought at him, my fingers curling into fists against the ground.

"Out loud, little mate," Edon told me.

"*Both*," I repeated.

"Good girl," he said, bending to capture one of my nipples between his teeth right as Silas sealed his mouth around my clit.

They worked me over in tandem with one another, fully in tune mentally and physically with my every need.

It was perfect.

Overwhelming.

Intoxicating.

Yet it wasn't enough. I needed so much more.

My veins *burned*, my stomach clenching as my insides pulsed with a craving only their cocks could satisfy. Yet Silas attempted to gratify me with his fingers, his movements nowhere near enough.

"*Please*," I panted, my body dancing on the edge of a magnificent plane that I couldn't quite reach. Their mouths and hands weren't going to take me there, just bring me right up to the precipice of ecstasy. "I need... I need..." I couldn't finish the statement, my lungs refusing to provide me with the air I required to speak.

It was too much.

Yet entirely insufficient.

More, more, more...

Edon switched breasts, his tongue laving my nipple, while Silas sucked on my sensitive nub. "How many fingers?" Edon asked softly.

"Four," Silas murmured. "She's fucking soaked, too."

"As she should be," Edon replied, his lips trailing up to meet mine in a kiss underlined in dark intent. I fell into his embrace, hypnotized by his dominance, craving his approval, reveling in his attention.

Silas and Edon both mastered me in different ways, their domination utterly complete while also being vastly distinctive.

They both submitted to me in certain instances, too.

It was an alluring dynamic, absolutely perfect in its uniqueness.

"Silas is going to sit up, and you're going to straddle him," Edon said against my mouth. "I want you to put his cock in your slick pussy and get him good and wet. Understand?"

I quivered, the mental image enough to make my inner walls spasm around Silas's fingers. *So close*, I thought, *I'm so damn close...*

"No coming until we're both inside you, little

mate," Edon told me as Silas's touch left my overheated sex. "Now go straddle our enforcer."

Both men disappeared, leaving me growling in their wake.

A feral need to *pounce* and *fuck* hit me square in the center of my abdomen, my gaze tracking their movements like a predator about to attack.

Only, they stared back at me with equal ferocity, making me realize it was their combined need that I was sensing via our bonds. Coupled with my own and it was a miracle I could still think clearly enough to move.

Silas slid fluidly to the ground, his cock an invitation between his legs I longed to claim. He went back to his elbows, his torso flexing with the movement, as he arched a single blond brow at me in silent challenge.

I went to my hands and knees and crawled toward him, my mouth watering at the sight of his damp tip. Rather than straddle him, I bent my head to take him into my mouth, his precum a decadent flavor on my tongue.

Edon's palm cracked across my ass, drawing a snarl from my inner beast. But his hands on my hips kept me from being able to swing around and swipe at him. "I told you to straddle him, not suck him off," he growled at me. "All our cum belongs in your cunt, Luna."

He grabbed a fistful of my hair to yank me up and

off Silas's dick, his lips suddenly at my ear as his hot chest pressed into my back.

"We're going to fucking breed you, little mate," he told me darkly. "Now do as you're told and *straddle Silas*."

He released me almost as suddenly as he'd grabbed me, causing me to fall forward.

Silas moved, catching me before I could tumble onto him. He issued a warning growl at the alpha behind me, which Edon responded to in kind.

Their aggression made me even wetter between my thighs, my inner wolf whining with intrinsic need. The sound escaped my mouth, only to be caught by Silas's tongue as he kissed me deeply, his hands guiding me into the position Edon had told me to assume.

Except Silas remained upright, his hard torso against my softer one, his hand on my nape as he worshipped my mouth.

"Put his cock inside you, Luna," Edon demanded, his dominance helping to ground me in the moment and anchor my thoughts.

Soon, I'd be reduced to an erotic mess of moans and whimpers.

I wanted at least a few moments of understanding, of *feeling* them taking me at the same time. Filling me completely. Driving me toward a climax unlike any we'd ever experienced. *Together as one.*

I wrapped my fingers around Silas's thick base and positioned him at my entrance.

He growled as I slid down, his hardness immediately satisfying my desire to be filled. Except his hands on my hips prevented me from moving the way I desired, his strength superior to mine. "*Silas*," I hissed.

"Not yet, little moon." His minty breath warmed my lips as he spoke, his body hard and muscular against mine. "Edon's going to prepare you to take more."

I moaned as the alpha in question blanketed my back with his heat, his mouth pressing a kiss to my shoulder as he slipped his hand over my rump.

While I knew what he intended to do, I still jolted as his finger rimmed my sex, his touch gliding alongside Silas's thick length as he entered me.

Fuck. I could feel my inner walls stretching, like my body was made for this, for *them*.

And it probably was.

Everything about our triad felt natural. Real. *Purposeful*.

We were a team. The perfect mates. So deeply in love with each other that nothing and no one could ever break us.

This is as it should be, I thought as Edon added a second finger.

Bringing a pup or two into the world with these males would be a dream come true.

We were safe.

Happy.

Finally at peace.

Our pack supported us. Respected us. Worked with us, not against us.

All of those who once supported Edon's father, Walter, were long gone.

Equality reigned in our pack.

It was the perfect place to create a family.

As we would now.

During my heat.

Edon added a third finger, his lips still pressed against my shoulder as Silas attempted to distract me with his tongue.

It worked, but the pressure was definitely building below. This would hurt at first, my channel not used to stretching to accommodate my mates in this manner.

"Relax, sweetheart," Edon said softly against my ear. "Just breathe."

I tried, but it was hard with Silas's mouth devouring mine. His palms ran up my abdomen to caress my breasts, his thumbs teasing my hard peaks while Edon continued to prepare me below.

Too much, I thought at him. *It… it's going to be… too much.*

"You can take us both," he whispered. "We'll be gentle at first. Work into a rhythm. Then we'll truly fuck you. Fill you with our cum over and over again."

Silas made a noise of anticipation that sounded a lot like a purr-induced growl, his chest vibrating mine. "I can't wait to see you growing with our child," he told me. "You're going to be so fucking sexy."

Edon murmured in agreement, adding, "We'll probably go into another rut just by looking at you."

My insides clenched at the thought, my heart skipping several beats.

Because I wanted that.

All of it.

With them.

"Ready, little mate?" Edon asked, his low voice sending a shiver down my spine.

Swallowing, I nodded, my head falling back to his shoulder as Silas rained kisses across my neck and throat.

"I'm going to ease in slowly," Edon told me, his thick head nudging my center.

Silas groaned at the sensation, clearly enjoying the sensual stroke.

Edon grasped my chin to pull me back toward him, his lips whispering across mine. "Breathe, sweetheart," he instructed, his command one I could better obey now that my mouth was mostly free.

Except I gasped more than inhaled, his thickness so much more intense than his fingers.

I immediately clamped down in response, my body wanting to reject the intrusion, but a growl from both of my mates had me melting instead, my sex somehow slickening even more.

Heat, I marveled. *Heat is a wondrous thing.*

Because it loosened my body, making me ready to *fuck.*

And it seemed to be greedily accepting both of my men now.

Oh, moons, I thought, dizzy from the sensation of being filled so completely. *I... I... Fuck!* A scream ripped from my mouth as Edon thrust all the way inside me, his girth stretching me and forcing me to take him and Silas.

Tears dampened my cheeks—tears that Edon chased with his tongue while Silas nuzzled my throat. Edon didn't release my chin, his lips still a hairsbreadth from mine as he studied my features, his dark eyes fathomless and intense.

He didn't move, just waited for me to acclimate.

All while Silas kissed and nipped at my neck, his touch sweet and sensual and exactly what I needed.

"You're doing so good, sweetheart," Edon praised me. "And you feel fucking incredible."

My insides spasmed in response to his words, my body primed and ready and so damn *hot.* "Please..."

"You want us to move, little moon?" Silas asked, his teeth skimming my pulse as he went to my ear. "Beg Edon. Tell him you want us to fuck you. To *breed* you."

His words stoked an inferno in my lower belly, one that had me moaning and writhing between them in response. "*Fuck,*" I managed on a breath. "I... I *need* you. Please."

"Hmm," Silas hummed, the vibration of his mouth against my ear making me tremble. "Be specific, darling Luna. *Beg* him."

I arched, my body trying to do the *begging* for me. But both men wouldn't move, their cocks lodged too deep to allow me much friction.

They were in charge.

Domineering.

Mine.

"*Breed me*," I growled at them. "Fuck me. Take me. Make me come. Help me lose my mind. *Fuck*. If you don't move, I—"

My words died on a moan as Edon moved inside me, his cock gliding out and back into me in a quick, harsh punch of his hips.

"More," I begged him. "Please, Edon. Please fuck me. Come inside me. Both of you. I... I can't... Just *move*... Please!"

He smiled against my mouth, his dark gaze capturing mine as my eyelashes fluttered open. I wasn't even sure when I'd closed my eyes, but it didn't matter now. I was captivated by his stare, his expression searing a new memory into my mind, one I would never forget.

One he punctuated by finally fucking *moving*.

Silas joined him, the two of them destroying me in absolutely the best way.

Fucking me.

Petting me.

Kissing me.

Edon went first, his tongue taming mine into submission, just for his hand on my chin to guide me to Silas's waiting mouth.

Hands were everywhere.

Teeth.

Lips.

Pleasure.

I practically vibrated between them, my body so pent up and alive that I couldn't think beyond the rapture caressing my core.

My mates' names left my mouth in sequence, their ministrations driving me closer and closer to a state of true oblivion.

Once I reached it, I'd lose touch with reality. Time. All sense of being.

Keep fucking me, I begged them. *Don't ever stop.*

We have no intention of stopping, little mate, Edon whispered back to me. *You're ours to cherish and fuck. And we're going to do exactly that.*

Love, too, Silas added. *Breed and love and worship.*

Yes, Edon agreed, his mouth positively savage against mine as he added, *Now come for us, little mate. I want to feel your pussy clench and throb around our shafts.*

Fuck, I breathed, losing complete control of my movements and of my mind.

I couldn't deny his commands.

I couldn't deny Silas's touch.

I couldn't deny Edon's mouth.

I couldn't deny their *cocks*.

It was all too much. And yet just right.

Perfect.

Beautiful.

Utterly stunning.

"*Now*," Edon demanded, that single word shooting me off into the heavens and allowing my heat to take over entirely.

Ecstasy chased me.

Need, my sole reason for being.

Fucking, my only source of existence.

I kissed my mates. Breathed them in. Reveled in their pleasure. Felt their warmth spill inside me. *Again and again.*

They tried new positions but always fucked me in unison, their cocks joining with my heat to create a whirlpool of pleasure.

So intense.

So *us*.

Edon bit my shoulder, marking me as his.

Silas bit my neck.

Their beasts were claiming me all over again, like we'd just joined for the first time. Except we'd been together for over a decade. Loving one another. Strengthening our triad.

But this was something else.

Something new.

Life.

I felt it flickering inside me.

A small warmth.

Creating. Thriving. Designing a future.

Our child.

It didn't matter who'd sired the new existence. Just like Edon had said, both men would be the father.

I could feel their elation.

Could feel their excitement.

Their devotion.

Their need to praise me as the mother of their future child.

Suddenly, their cocks were replaced with tongues. Fingers. Hands. Worshipping. Caressing. *Loving*.

At some point, they'd moved me to a bed.

I was only vaguely aware of the mattress beneath me yet fully cognizant of their mouths. Licking. Sucking. Drawing out my pleasure.

Words of adoration filtered through my thoughts.

My mates were pleased. They loved me. Loved *us*. And they were going to ensure the little one growing inside me would know it, too.

Our triad was about to become a family of four.

"Five," Edon corrected against my ear.

I blinked, the world starting to resurface around me. "Hmm?"

"Five," he repeated. "A family of five."

My brow furrowed, only to be smoothed out by Silas's thumb as he chuckled against my opposite side. "Twins, Luna."

I blinked again. *Twins?*

"Can't you feel it?" Edon asked, his palm on my belly. "Two lives, little mate."

Silas's hand covered his. "Two children."

"A family of five," Edon echoed as he nuzzled my neck. "You're amazing, Luna."

"Our gorgeous mate," Silas added in a whisper. "We love you, little moon. And we love the growing lives inside you, too."

I laid my hand over both of theirs, my instincts drifting inward as I tried to discern what they already knew.

And sure enough, I immediately sensed it.

Not one, but two.

Twins, I thought once more, only this time I understood.

My lips curled. "A family of five."

Edon chuckled. "Yes, sweetheart." He brushed a kiss against my cheek. "And I know just how we should celebrate…"

My legs instantly wanted to close, my body sore from however long we'd been fucking.

"Pancakes," Silas said, causing my eyes to blink yet again.

"Pancakes," Edon agreed.

"Take care of our mate while I cook," Silas told Edon.

"Oh, I'll take care of her all right." Edon's palm flexed against my abdomen.

But just as I thought he intended to begin another round, he scooped me up into his arms and carried me to a waiting bath.

I inhaled the fresh aroma, wondering when and how they'd put this together.

However, then I decided I didn't care.

Because this was my home.

My haven.

My life.

Stroking my abdomen, I smiled. *And this is our future...*

Meanwhile, Decades Later…

Ismerelda? Cam's voice in my head had me stopping midstep. *Why are you in the catacombs?*

My lips twisted to the side as I determined how to respond to that.

He could already hear in my head why I'd ventured underground, but he clearly didn't fully understand my reasoning.

Likely because I didn't really know either.

Something… I trailed off. *I had a weird dream.*

And that dream was followed by this strange urge to go underground.

A bizarre desire, considering I hadn't been down here in years.

Cam and I had completely renovated Rome and Vatican City, though we hadn't touched much of what existed down here. Mostly because we didn't want to disturb the Blessed Ones resting in the tombs, or the mortal remains.

We also didn't have much of a use for the abandoned labs and cages in Cane's former bunker.

Instead, we'd focused on rebuilding the outside.

It'd taken decades to complete our vision—which had primarily been *my* vision, but that was because Cam had wanted me to make the land my version of a utopia.

Which I had with the help of other regions, such as Khalid Region and Jace Region. They had resources we'd needed to take down all of Lilith's and Cane's old buildings and create from the ground up.

Our new home didn't resemble old Rome or Vatican City at all, but instead consisted of glass-like structures, ample trees and wildlife, and energy-efficient housing.

The humans who lived within our boundaries seemed to thrive, their skill sets fundamentally focused in engineering and farming to help us sustain life without needing to trade much with others.

Of course, we still traded with our allies.

But for the most part, we were a self-sustainable society of vampires, lycans, and immortal humans.

The blood tax was minimal and just enough to keep the vampires alive.

And the lycans who resided here had been carefully vetted by Cam, primarily because they were rogue wolves who had chosen to leave their clans.

Everyone in this new world had a *fend for yourself*

mentality, which worked for some but didn't for others.

Hence the reason Cam was currently focused on our region's security.

He and Khalid were building some sort of invisible barrier meant to protect the borders. I didn't fully understand the technology.

Ismerelda, Cam said again.

I'm fine, I told him, sensing his concern. *I'm your queen, remember?*

Oh, I remember, he murmured back to me. *My stubborn lioness. What was the phrase, though? The one you taught me recently? Something about curiosity and a cat?*

I snorted. *That doesn't apply to—*

A giggle had me freezing in place and put Cam instantly on alert in my head.

Get out now, he demanded.

While part of me understood his abrupt command, another part of me was too drawn to that unexpected sound to do what he'd ordered me to do.

Primarily because that sound was one I'd heard in my dream last night.

Ismerelda. I could feel Cam phasing back to the catacombs while he growled my name.

I was about to reply when a female stepped into my path, her gold irises flaring wide upon seeing me. A male joined at her side, his expression shifting from amused to guarded in a second.

"Oh, hello," the female greeted, her voice—*and face*—matching my dream.

I pinched my side, wondering if perhaps I was still somehow asleep.

She cocked her head, her long, dark hair falling over her shimmering gown—a gown that reminded me of a glittering star. "You're a unique vampire." She canted her head the other way. "A mated vampire." She glanced at her companion. "Do you feel it?"

"Yes." His single-word reply was terse, his black-rimmed silver eyes riddled with distrust. The look reminded me of Cam.

The female danced forward—*danced* because I couldn't describe it as *walking*. She was practically floating over the ground, her sandal-like footwear weaving up her calves in delicate gold ribbons.

"Nyx," the male warned as his female counterpart stepped within a foot of my frozen form.

Nyx? I repeated to myself, dumbfounded. *Like… like, the Nyx? The Goddess of Vampires Nyx?*

Cam's presence warmed my back in the next instant, his body seeming to materialize beside me. But instead of his sudden appearance startling the female before me, she simply stared at him with interest.

The male behind her, however, narrowed his gaze, clearly displeased by Cam's abrupt arrival.

"You must be Cronus's son," Nyx said, looking Cam up and down. "You look just like him. Which means…" Those golden eyes went back to me. "You're this one's mate?"

"Y-yes," I managed to reply.

Nyx—*holy fuck, I'm standing in front of a fucking goddess*—clapped her hands and spun toward the male. "Oh, Vesperus, isn't this wonderful?"

"That remains to be seen," he returned, his attention entirely on Cam. "Are we going to have a problem here?"

Goddess Nyx. Cam… I dreamt of her last night. And she's… she's Goddess Nyx.

I know, he replied, his palm finding my lower back. "Were you asleep somewhere in the catacombs?" he asked, ignoring Vesperus's query entirely. "Or did you… just arrive?"

Nyx glanced at him and then at Vesperus. "Catacombs?"

"It seems we woke up in a crypt underground," Vesperus murmured to her, answering her and Cam's questions at the same time. "That's definitely not where we fell asleep."

"We were in a cave," she murmured. "I suppose perhaps the world created new layers around us?"

"Perhaps," he replied. "Your magic would have protected us."

"Yes," she agreed, her palm unfolding to display a pile of glittery dust.

The air around us rippled as two new arrivals joined us underground. *Khalid and Emine.*

Nyx glanced at them, her lips instantly curling. "Ah, Erinas." Her smile slipped then, her brow furrowing. "No. Erinas's son." She glanced at Emine.

"And you... you are not a vampire." She studied Emine intently. "You are quite fascinating."

"She is," Khalid agreed before anyone else could speak. Then he bowed slightly, showing the female respect. "Goddess Nyx."

Nyx sighed. "See, King. This is what I'm used to. So much better than being shot at, yes?"

Vesperus's lips twitched. "Yes, Goddess."

"Well." She clasped her hands before her. "Would any of you like to give us a tour of the world? I'd love to see what's become of my gifts."

Cam and I shared a look.

"We would love to," Khalid said, volunteering before Cam and I could finish processing Nyx's request. "We'll start in Blood City."

"Blood City?" Nyx repeated.

Khalid smiled. "Yes. It's the heart of the past, present, and future. I suspect you'll be quite pleased with what you'll find there..."

The End...
For now.

CONCLUSION

THANK YOU SO MUCH FOR PLAYING INSIDE MY MIND!

I hope you enjoyed the Blood Alliance series as much as I did. It's been quite the journey. I can't wait to continue writing in that world in the future.

That said, *Blood City* will be next, and I intend to write it as two parts. Part One will likely overlap with *Blood Day*, as I want to explore Emine and Khalid's meet-cute (writer speak for "how they met").

Part Two will take place at an undetermined time. It depends on where my muse and the voices take me. Khalid and Emine have a lot to say. It's going to be fun!

Please join Foss's Night Owls for the most up-to-date release information. That's where you can find me online. However, I also send updates via my newsletter for those who prefer to avoid social media.

Hugs to you!

Lexi

BLOOD DAY - A STANDALONE BLOOD UNIVERSITY DUET

Blood Day.
The deadly graduation ceremony that dictates who I
will become in this world run by vampires and lycans.

There is no escape. Nowhere to run. Obey or die.

My name isn't relevant. My identity fails to mean a
thing. It's my scores that count. And Master Cedric is
hell-bent on failing me.

I bow. I beg. I crawl.
But nothing is good enough for the ancient vampire

with cruel dark eyes. He wants me to bleed exclusively for him. Yet that's not how this society works.

I can't fail. My life depends on it.
I will fight until my last breath. Even if that means dying on my knees before the vampire god who rules my classroom.

Welcome to the future where the superior bloodlines make the rules.
You're about to enter the Blood University world, where humans have no rights. No choices. And there are no second chances. Proceed at your own risk.

CRAVE ME - A STANDALONE PARANORMAL ROMANCE

Once upon a time, a series of portals opened on Earth, allowing magic to spill into the human world.
Houses were created. Supernaturals were assigned. And a new balance was formed.
All new arrivals are required to join a House.
But this is the tale of a goddess who refused and the House King who brought her to heel.

Nyx.
Goddess of Night.
My newest obsession.

The daring female killed one of my men.

Which made it my job as the Gold and Garnet House King to make her pay.

Oh, there were so many things I wanted to do with that disobedient little mouth of hers. But she was much stronger than she led anyone to believe. Now I'm left with a craving I can't quite sate. Because one bite wasn't enough.

You may be the Goddess of Night, but I'm still your king.
You will kneel.
You will beg.
And most importantly, you will bleed.

Welcome to the House of Gold and Garnet, where power defines the monarchy and blood is a preferred currency.
Proceed at your own risk.

Author's Note: *Crave Me* is a dark standalone paranormal romance set in the Immortal Vices and Virtues Universe. Every book in this shared world is a guaranteed happily-ever-after with a satisfying ending and no cliffhangers.

For fans of the Blood Alliance series, this is the story of Nyx and Vesperus, the goddess and her vampire lover that started it all...

USA Today Bestselling Author Lexi C. Foss loves to play in dark worlds, especially the ones that bite. She lives in North Carolina with her family. When not writing, she's busy crossing items off her travel bucket list, or chasing eclipses around the globe. She's quirky, consumes way too much coffee, and loves to swim.

Want access to the most up-to-date information for all of Lexi's books? Sign-up for her newsletter here.

Lexi also likes to hang out with readers on Facebook in her exclusive readers group - Join Here.

Where To Find Lexi:
www.LexiCFoss.com

ALSO BY LEXI C. FOSS

Blood Alliance Series - Dystopian Paranormal

Chastely Bitten

Royally Bitten

Regally Bitten

Rebel Bitten

Kingly Bitten

Cruelly Bitten

Blood Alliance Standalones - Dystopian Paranormal

Blood Day

Blood City

Crave Me

Frost Bitten

Dark Provenance Series - Paranormal Romance

Heiress of Bael (FREE!)

Daughter of Death

Son of Chaos

Paramour of Sin

Princess of Bael

Captive of Hell

Elemental Fae Academy - Reverse Harem

Book One

Book Two

Book Three

Elemental Fae Queen

Winter Fae Queen

Hell Fae - Reverse Harem

Hell Fae Captive

Hell Fae Warden

Hell Fae Commander

Hell Fae Prince

Hell Fae King

Immortal Curse Series - Paranormal Romance

Book One: Blood Laws

Book Two: Forbidden Bonds

Book Three: Blood Heart

Book Four: Blood Bonds

Book Five: Angel Bonds

Book Six: Blood Seeker

Book Seven: Wicked Bonds

Book Eight: Blood King

Immortal Curse World - Short Stories & Bonus Fun

Elder Bonds

Blood Burden

Assassin Bonds

Mershano Empire Series - Contemporary Romance

Book One: The Prince's Game

Book Two: The Charmer's Gambit

Book Three: The Rebel's Redemption

Midnight Fae Academy - Reverse Harem

Ella's Masquerade

Book One

Book Two

Book Three

Book Four

Nightmare Fae - Reverse Harem

Their Lethal Pet

Noir Reformatory - Ménage Paranormal Romance

The Beginning

First Offense

Second Offense

Third Offense

Fourth Offense

Underworld Royals Series - Dark Paranormal Romance

Happily Ever Crowned

Happily Ever Bitten

X-Clan Series - Dystopian Paranormal

X-Clan: The Origin

Andorra Sector

X-Clan: The Experiment

Winter's Arrow

Bariloche Sector

V-Clan Series - Dystopian Paranormal

Blood Sector

Night Sector

Eclipse Sector

Vampire Dynasty - Dark Paranormal

Violet Slays

Crossed Fates

Other Books

Scarlet Mark - Standalone Romantic Suspense

Rotanev - Standalone Poseidon Tale

Carnage Island - Standalone Reverse Harem Romance

Monsterland Mayhem - Standalone Reverse Harem Romance

Claim Me - Standalone Reverse Harem Romance

Chase Me - Standalone Omegaverse Romance

www.ingramcontent.com/pod-product-compliance
Lightning Source LLC
Chambersburg PA
CBHW020319130626
46549CB00003B/929